THE PENGUIN POETS

GOD HUNGER

Michael Ryan's first volume of poetry, *Threats Instead of Trees*, won the Yale Series of Younger Poets Award and was nominated for a National Book Award in 1974. His second volume, *In Winter*, was a selection in the National Poetry Series in 1981. He has received many other awards for his poetry, including a Guggenheim Fellowship, two fellowships from the National Endowment for the Arts, and a Whiting Writers' Award. He teaches in the MFA Program for Writers at Warren Wilson College and lives in Charlottesville, Virginia.

God Hunger

Also by Michael Ryan

Threats Instead of Trees
In Winter

GOD HUNGER

Poems by Michael Ryan

PENGUIN BOOKS

PENGUIN BOOKS
Published by the Penguin Group
Viking Penguin, a division of Penguin Books USA Inc.,
375 Hudson Street, New York, New York 10014, U.S.A.
Penguin Books Ltd, 27 Wrights Lane,
London W8 5TZ, England
Penguin Books Australia Ltd, Ringwood,
Victoria, Australia
Penguin Books Canada Ltd, 2801 John Street,
Markham, Ontario, Canada L3R 1B4
Penguin Books (N.Z.) Ltd, 182–190 Wairau Road,
Auckland 10, New Zealand

Penguin Books Ltd, Registered Offices:
Harmondsworth, Middlesex, England

First published in the United States of America by
Viking Penguin, a division of Penguin Books
USA Inc., 1989
Published in Penguin Books 1990

1   3   5   7   9   10   8   6   4   2

Copyright © Michael Ryan, 1989
All rights reserved

Page vii constitutes an extension of the copyright page.

LIBRARY OF CONGRESS CATALOGING IN PUBLICATION DATA
Ryan, Michael.
God hunger: poems/by Michael Ryan.
p.   cm.
ISBN 0 14 058.620 2
I. Title.
[PS3568.Y39G64   1990]
811'.54—dc20   89–78394

Printed in the United States of America
Set in Bembo
Designed by Francesca Belanger

Except in the United States of America, this
book is sold subject to the condition that it
shall not, by way of trade or otherwise, be lent,
re-sold, hired out, or otherwise circulated
without the publisher's prior consent in any form
of binding or cover other than that in which it
is published and without a similar condition
including this condition being imposed on the
subsequent purchaser.

ACKNOWLEDGMENTS

Thanks to the editors of the magazines in which the following poems first appeared:

American Poetry Review: Blue Corridor, The Crown of Frogs, First Exercise, The Gladiator, God Hunger, Her Report, Moonlight, Not the End of the World, One, Passion, Portrait of a Lady, A Postcard from Italy, Sea Worms, Spider Plant, A Splinter, TV Room at the Children's Hospice, Two Rides on a Bike
The Nation: Crossroads Inn, Milk the Mouse
The New Republic: This Is Why
The New Yorker: Fire, My Dream by Henry James, Switchblade, Tourists on Paros
Ploughshares: A Burglary
Poetry: County Fair, Larkinesque, The Past, Tanglewood, Winter Drought
The Threepenny Review: The Ditch, Smoke
TriQuarterly: "Boy 'Carrying-In' Bottles in Glass Works," Pedestrian Pastoral, Stone Paperweight, Through a Crack
Virginia Quarterly Review: Houseflies, Meeting Cheever

Thanks also to the John Simon Guggenheim Memorial Foundation, the National Endowment for the Arts, the Virginia Commission for the Arts, the Mrs. Giles Whiting Foundation, and the Corporation of Yaddo for their generous support during the years I worked on this book.

And love and thanks to Stephen Berg, Louise Glück, Stanley Kunitz, and Ellen Bryant Voigt for their responses to these poems in manuscript.

for Debra Nystrom

CONTENTS

God Hunger

NOT THE END OF THE WORLD

What flew down the chimney
into the cold wood stove
in my study? Wings
alive inside cast iron
gave the cold stove a soul
wilder than fire, in trouble.
I knocked the window-screen out
with a hand-heel's thunk,
and dropped the shade over
the top half of the window,
and shut the study door,
and wadded the keyhole,
hoping whatever it was
would fly for the light,
the full, clean stream of light
like the sliding board from heaven
our guardian angels slid to earth on
in *The Little Catholic Messenger*
weekly magazine. I genuflected once,
but only to flick the stove-latch
and spring behind a bookcase
through a memory-flash
of church-darkness, incense-smoke
mushrooming as the censer
clanks and swings back
toward the Living Host
in His golden cabinet.
A dull brown bird no bigger
than my fist hopped modestly

out, twisting its neck like a boxer
trying to shake off a flush punch.
And there on my rug, dazed,
heedless of the spotlight, it stayed,
and stayed, then settled down
as if to hatch an egg it was hallucinating.
So I scooped it into my two hands,
crazed heart in a feathered ounce,
and sat it outside on the dirt.

And there I left it.
It didn't even try its wings,
not one perfunctory flap,
but staggered a few rickety steps
before collapsing, puffing its tiny bulk.
I watched behind a window
other identical little dull birds
land within inches and chart
circles around it. Five of them,
cheeping, chased an inquiring cat.
Then all of them one by one—
by this time, a dozen—mounted its back
and fluttered jerkily like helicopters
trying to unbog a truck,
and, when that didn't work,
pecked it and pecked it,
a gust of flicks, to kill it
or rouse it I couldn't tell

until they all stepped back to wait.
It flapped once and fell forward
and rested its forehead on the ground.

I've never seen such weakness.
I thought to bring it back in
or call someone, but heard my voice
saying, "Birds die, we all die,"
the shock of being picked up again
would probably finish it,
so with this pronouncement
I tried to clear it from my mind
and return to the work I had waiting
that is most of what I can do
even if it changes nothing.

Do I need to say I was away
for all of a minute
before I went back to it?
But the bird was gone.
All the birds were gone,
and the circle they had made
now made a space so desolate
that for one moment I saw
the dead planet.

MY DREAM BY HENRY JAMES

In my dream by Henry James there is a sentence:
"Stay and comfort your sea companion
for a while," spoken by an aging man
to a young one as they dawdle on the terrace
of a beachfront hotel. The young man doesn't know
how to feel—which is often the problem
in James, which may have been the problem
with James, living, as he said, *in* the work
("this is the only thing"), shaping his late
concerti of almost inaudible ephemerae
on the emotional scale. By 1980,
when this dream came to me, the line spoken
takes on sexual overtones, especially since
as the aging man says it he earnestly presses
the young man's forearm, and in James
no exchange between people is simple,
but the young man turns without answering
to gaze over the balustrade at the ocean,
over the pastel textures of beach umbrellas
and scalloped dresses whose hems brush the sand,
without guessing the aging man's loneliness
and desire for him. He sees only monotony
as he watches waves coming in, and this odd
old man who shared his parents' table on the ship
seems the merest disturbance of the air,
a mayfly at such distance he does not quite hear.
Why should I talk to anyone? glides over his mind
like a cloud above a pond
that mirrors what passes over and does not remember.

But I remember this cloud and this pond
from a mid-week picnic with my mother
when I was still too little for school
and we were alone together
darkened by shadows of pines
when with both hands she turned my face
toward the cloud captured in the water
and everything I felt in the world was love for her.

THIS IS WHY

He will never be given to wonder much
if he was the mouth for some cruel force
that said it. But if he were
(this will comfort her) less than one moment
out of millions had he meant it.

So many years and so many turns
they had swerved around the subject.
And he will swear for many more
the kitchen and everything in it vanished—

the oak table, their guests, the refrigerator door
he had been surely propped against—
all changed to rusted ironwork and ash
except in the center in her linen caftan:
she was not touched.

He remembers the silence before he spoke
and her nodding a little,
as if in the meat of this gray waste
here was the signal

for him to speak what they had long agreed,
what somewhere they had prepared together.
And this one moment in the desert of ash
stretches into forever.

They had been having a dinner party.
She had been lonely.

A friend asked her almost joking
if she had ever felt really crazy,

and when she started to unwind her answer
in long, lovely sentences like scarves within her
he saw that this was the way
they could no longer talk together.

And that is when he said it,
in front of the guests,
because he couldn't bear to hear her.
And this is why the guests have left
and she screams as he comes near her.

TV ROOM AT
THE CHILDREN'S HOSPICE

Red-and-green leather-helmeted
maniacally grinning motorcyclists
crash at all angles
on Lev Smith's pajama top

and when his chocolate ice cream
dumps like a mud slide down its front
he smiles, not maniacally, still nauseous
from chemotherapy and bald already.

Lev is six but sat still four hours
all afternoon with IVs in his arms,
his grandma tells everyone. Marcie
is nine and was born with no face.

One profile has been built in increments
with surgical plastic and skin grafts
and the other looks like fudge.
Tomorrow she's having an eye moved.

She finds a hand-mirror in the toy box
and maybe for the minute I watch
she sees nothing she doesn't expect.
Ruth Borthnott's son, Richard,

cracked his second vertebra
at diving practice eight weeks ago,
and as Ruth describes getting the news
by telephone (shampoo suds plopped

all over the notepad she tried
to write on) she smiles like Lev Smith
at his ice cream, smiles also saying
Richard's on a breathing machine,

if he makes it he'll be quadriplegic,
she's there in intensive care every day
at dawn. The gameshow-shrill details
of a Hawaiian vacation for two

and surf teasing the ankles
of the couple on a moonlit beachwalk
keep drawing her attention
away from our conversation.

I say it's amazing how life can change
from one second to the next,
and with no apparent disdain
for this dismal platitude,

she nods yes, and yes again
at the gameshow's svelte assistant
petting a dinette set, and yes
to Lev Smith's grandma

who has appeared beside her
with microwaved popcorn
blooming like a huge
cauliflower from its tin.

THE GLADIATOR

*a tintinnabula apparently used
in Dionysiac rituals*
　　　—Erotic Art of Pompeii

His cock is bigger than he is
and thickens out from his thighs
until it touches earth and curls
back to attack him with a mad dog's head:
jaws stretched, bared teeth, going for his throat.
Maybe the craftsman meant only to tell us
something simple through rough humor,
but the gladiator's countenance
radiates a madonna's calm
as the raised sword in his right hand
poises to chop down this thing grown from him
the instant its teeth will crush his neck,
and he just looks beyond it
at some miracle invisible to us.
The monstrosity, on the contrary,
seems gorged with anguish, with all
the anguish of this moment of no-time
it would kill everything to end.
Is this the punishment for being a man
who woke to see the evil he had become?
Or the defeat at the bottom of the self
exactly imagined, banished
by the sexual ritual of the bells?

MILK THE MOUSE

He'll pinch my pinky until the mouse starts squeaking.
The floorlamp casts a halo around his big, stuffed chair.
Be strong Be tough! It is my father speaking.

I'm four or five. Was he already drinking?
With its tip and knuckle between his thumb and finger,
he'll pinch my pinky until the mouse starts squeaking

Stop, Daddy, stop (it was more like screeching)
and kneels down before him on the hardwood floor.
Be strong Be tough! It is my father speaking.

What happened to him that he'd do such a thing?
It's only a game, he's doing me a favor
to pinch my pinky until the mouse starts squeaking

because the world will run over a weakling
and we must crush the mouse or be crushed later.
Be strong Be tough! It was my father speaking

to himself, of course, to the child inside him aching,
not to me. But how can I not go when he calls me over
to pinch my pinky until the mouse starts squeaking
Be strong Be tough? It is my father speaking.

MEETING CHEEVER

Iowa City, 1973

Above a half pizza and double gin,
his proffered hand trembled in the dark
as if, polished and slapped with cologne,
he had ridden a jackhammer from New York

that broke up everything inside
but politesse, which dangled like a hook:
informed you had just won a prize,
he said, "Ah yes, I loved your book."

And you, inconsolable bell-bottomed cliché
of wounded-by-the-world angry young poet
who became me as strangely as years become today,
replied, "The book's not published yet."

In a booth for four were mashed five
whose egos would have cramped the Astrodome.
One thriving now, who still tries
to disguise his voice answering the phone

from decades of throwing bill collectors off,
whose wife told everyone her life was hell,
whose children had it rough,
was living by the week in a seedy motel.

He had killed a quart by noon
with a mountainous hard-boiled novelist
who thought Chandler "could write circles around *anyone*
with a piece of chalk in his ass."

12

Ungoaded, Cheever smiled at the figure
and said he'd love to see *that* manuscript.
Pinned between them, ankle to shoulder,
he looked like a sandwiched Siamese triplet

twice their age and half their size
but sharing one bloodstream—alcohol—
and one passion beyond themselves: stories
wild, precise, and beautiful.

My counterpart in the art of verse
was burbling his soda through a straw.
"Consciousness is a curse"
and "Coke-farts evoke sacred awe"

were his night's remarks, not addressed to us.
His poems were tiny nests of pain.
That Christmas he went to Panama in a VW bus
and no one ever saw him again.

And the hard-boiled novelist's new baby and wife,
then unconceived and not-yet-met,
that were said to have filled his life
with happiness and made him considerate,

died together in a crash.
Where was this future with its bloody claws?
Brilliant John Cheever is a handful of ash.
I would be finished with what I was.

"BOY 'CARRYING-IN' BOTTLES IN GLASS WORKS"

West Virginia, 1911
Photograph by Lewis W. Hine

What makes his face heartbreaking
is that he wouldn't have it so—
just one of many boys working
amid splinters of glass that throw
such light they seem its only source
in this dusky photograph.
A random instant of the past.
And the brutal factory, of course,

is only one memory of brutality
on the world's infinite list.
The boy would now be over eighty,
retired, unnoticed,
but surely he was stunted and is dead.
It's this look of his—
like a word almost said—
across an unchartable distance,

that shapes and bends
emotion toward him now,
though he wouldn't have it so.
He just looked into a lens
amid splinters of glass that throw
such light they seem its only source,
and rods and chutes that criss-cross
like some malign, unnameable force.

WINTER DROUGHT

P. K. (1957–1977)

First you cut your wrists and throat,
then after they had sewn you up,
after three months of hospitals and talk,
after those who loved you cried themselves out
and their faces changed to sculptures of mistrust
in the early light, in the breakfast nook,
as you told them each day point-blank
how you felt about this life,
after they could no longer answer or look up,
you stole your father's car and drove it
to the bridge across the bay near Jamestown
where the police found it three days before
they found your body, bloated and frozen.
How could anyone so young want to die
so much? we asked, as if loneliness
tightened its death-grip gradually with age;
but we felt much older and lonelier ourselves
for a few days, until your terrible final image
began to fade and even your close friends
became again content enough
in that vast part of life
with families and earthly concerns
where your absence had never been noticed.
Such were the limits of friendship
you railed against, cursing its "ersatz intimacy"
one evening after a reading: in a crummy Cambridge bar,
with our uncomfortable group of ten
trapped in a half-moon booth,
you climbed onto the table and screamed,

and we heard you and could do nothing
but pick up broken glass and take you home.

Now it has been years.
You were nearly nothing to me—a friend
of a friend, a pushy kid who loved poetry,
one more young man alone in his distress—
but last week when I went out to where I sometimes walk,
across a field of chopped stalks yellowed and dried
by months of snowless winter,
you rose abruptly from the undercurrents of memory
dredged in a steel net, and I was there
where I never was, amid boat noise
and ocean stink, your corpse
twisting as if hurt
when the net broke the surface,
then riding toward me, motionless
pale blue against the water's black.
And I've seen you here every day since,
as if I were walking the beach
the moment you balance on the iced, iron railing
and jump. Does such rage for pain
give immaculate clarity to things?
Like winter sunlight day after day
showing this field for what it is:
dust and splintered stalks
about to become dust?
Tell me what you want.

SPIDER PLANT

When I opened my eyes this morning,
the fact of its shooting out
long thin green runners on which miniatures
of the mother will sprout,
and that each of these offshoots
could in its own time repeat this,
terrified me. And something seemed awful
in the syllables of the word "Brenda,"
sounding inside me before they made a name,
then making a name of no one I've known.
I had been dreaming I was married to Patty
again. She kept coming on my tongue
and I knew if I put myself in
we'd have to stay together this time.
But I wanted to, and did, and as I did
the sadness and pleasure of our nine years together
washed through me as a river, yet
I knew this wasn't right, it couldn't
work, and though we were now enmeshed
forever, I began to rise from my body
making love with her on the bed and to hover
at a little distance over both of us.
That's when I awoke and saw the spider plant.

TWO RIDES ON A BIKE

1

A seventy-degree day in February!,
the air a gentle rapture on the skin,
so I forgot everything else
and pedalled to the pond on a blacktop
that lies across the modest dips and rises of Virginia,
past empty half-pints of Wild Rose,
Burger King wrappers, wafers of black ice
in the intricate, multi-shadowed underbrush,
past crushed skunks on the shoulders,
months of roadkill, unidentifiable,
dwindled to fur clumps and greasespots,
past vultures scared into the air,
into wide, weaving helixes
above a cluster of white-muzzled holsteins
each wearing a single green plastic earring
as if waiting for the limo of some punk rocker,
a numbered tag like the kind we get to mark
our place in line at a busy deli or car wash,
all regarding me as placidly as pashas
as I coasted down to the pond
with the four-by-four-foot wooded island in it
you call my mini-Innisfree.
Because the sun was diamonds on the water,
I didn't notice at first the gaggle of Canada geese
gathered near the spot we sometimes sit in summer
to talk things out when the walls of our house—
who knows why?—become impediments.

A gander honked as I approached,
and kept honking as I parked the bike,
a cry that anything breathing could recognize
as warning or distress, but since all the geese
had already launched into the water and paddled
to the middle of the pond, I couldn't understand
why he didn't just go in with them and shut up.
Then I saw the source of the fuss:
one goose alone on the island
fixated on me, her neck extended and tensed.
Do geese nest in February? Whatever the reason
she was out there by herself, I sat down anyway
on the bank, quieting the gander
now gliding between me and the island
back and forth like a toy patrol boat.
In the silence I soon lost myself
as I had hoped to in being in that place,
the off-white mat of grass
a generous cushion, the trees' stripped skeletons
lining the shore like watchmen
in an ancient Chinese emperor's tomb,
the water, as I said, glittering,
and, only a yard away—between me and this dazzling—
reddish-brown marsh grass, rich amber,
the color of your hair in summer.
When I reached to feel its texture,
that damned gander began honking again
and the goose choked a low sound from her throat

as she stepped off the island to meet him
and swim elsewhere—since, whatever wonders
we may be to ourselves or to each other, to them
we're only harm and danger.

2

When I see wild raspberries
on a thorny vine that arcs
like a question mark out of the woods
and sways almost imperceptibly
above the edge of the crunching
gravel road I ride my bike on
needing to be far from any sort of traffic,
I assume they may be sprayed
with one of those toxic nightmares
agribusiness concocted of the naive dream
of getting something for nothing from the earth.
Glistening, resolutely silent, plump
as a thumb joint, nearly splitting
with ripeness, not of the world
where people wake choking on poison gas,
their fruit-meat laced with indigestible seeds
replanted in the droppings of animals
nourished in a cycle of mutual survival,
they do evoke fantasies of Eden.
But I left them where they were
after testing their delicate heft
on my fingertips, and when I knocked

the kickstand up, I might
have heard a voice from my past
or even from another life, but no,
it was just the wild raspberries
snug in their lusciousness.

THROUGH A CRACK

That bird's odd chirp behind the fence
I thought the rasp of garden shears
I used as a boy to edge the lawn
late Saturday afternoon for years.

The neighborhood was quiet then.
The shades drawn tight against the heat.
The lawns all done, the bushes trimmed.
No sound but this escaped the street:

not Dougherty's incandescent, yattering TV,
not Galliano's shrieking fights,
not Quigley's muted .22
pinking rabbits from his bedroom by moonlight:

only the red, padded handles in my grip
and the stubby spring released and squeezed
and the *chik chik* of blue steel blades
as I inched along the border on my knees.

SEA WORMS

"Exotic Organisms Found In Pacific Ocean"
—The New York Times

In sulfurous plumes of water
from vents in the bottom crust,
new life continually forms
and thrives on what would kill us,

so maybe when you plunge
into your black, internal pit
something lovely and strange
will emerge from it.

Five-foot red-headed sea worms
that peek out of tubes they live in
don't look exactly in the photo
like rampant uncircumcision,

nor was the oceanographer kidding
describing that underworld scene
"like driving through a wheat field
in a submarine,"

but I tried to make it a joke
because I wanted you to laugh,
because I couldn't touch you,
because my love was useless,

because Chekhov was right—
"the soul of another lies in darkness"—
though I feel your cells call to mine
across the abyss of inches between us

when we lie in darkness together,
your luminous eyes wide open,
three miles deep in yourself
rooted in poison.

THE PAST

It shows up one summer in a greatcoat,
storms through the house confiscating,
says it must be paid and quickly,
says it must take everything.

Your children stare into their cornflakes,
your wife whispers only once to stop it
because she loves you and she sees it
darken the room suddenly like a stain.

What did you do to deserve it,
ruining breakfast on a balmy day?
Kiss your loved ones. Night is coming.
There was no life without it anyway.

HER REPORT

When the little three-note computer tune
played faster and louder inside my heart,
if I didn't get the straitjacket on
my body would start flying apart.

But I never stopped caring what was thought
of someone who asked to be strapped down,
so I'd wait and wait and wait
and wait, until I became no one

and nothing bad could happen to me
or to anyone I had loved this hard
and they all paraded like a line of trees
seen from a carriage on a boulevard.

You were there. I saw you there.
Closer to me than you are now.
Light unobstructed by the air
showed me your feelings inside out—

the deepest ones most stunningly clear,
the ugly pain that's yours alone
I suddenly understood, and loved you for.
Then your face flicked past. You were gone.

Nothing I can tell you now
will say how much I missed you then.
I thought I was dying, yet all I cared about
was that I would never see you again.

A BURGLARY

It was only of my studio at Yaddo,
a twenty-by-twenty cabin in the woods
whose walls are nearly all windows,
and all they got was a typewriter and stereo
(I say "they" though it may have been one burglar)
and something ludicrously cheap, like a stapler,
I didn't miss at first and now can't remember,
though I remember my not being able to find the thing weeks later
bringing the fact of the burglary back in a rush.
A discontinued Smith-Corona, a decent stereo, maybe a stapler,
and a goose-neck desk lamp that belonged to Yaddo,
whereas next to the lamp on the desk, untouched,
were my bankbook and checkbook in full view.
The detective said, "This tells you they're pros."
(He said "they," too.) But maybe partly from seeing
so many paintings that summer,
the desk-top with familiar objects removed
fixed into a still life: bankbook and checkbook
placed just so—blue analogous rectangles
rounding at the corners, miniature glazed deep pools,
and inside them whole schools of frantic ink numbers
suspended within such stolid form and color
they became flimsy and funny, a Duchamp joke, arbitrary,
the representation of what no one sees.
Also, the burglar(s) had slashed the screen
into an inverted V that was sticking into the room like a tongue,
and had jimmied the window open
while the door was unlocked all along.
"Maybe this is actually a Happening," I said and laughed

with a sound like someone else clearing his throat.
I can still see the detective tiredly scrutinizing my face
in the melting light of evening
a cross-draft seemed to wash in waves through the cabin
during the endless seconds before he asked, "What's that?"

All the Yaddo staff and most of the guests
offered regrets appropriate to a loss
which even to me did not sound great
within the world's constant howl of misery—
plague and catastrophe featured nightly on TV,
the zillion sirens heard in a lifetime
each naming horror for someone.
When word of the burglary skittered through the dining room
(like a dropped glass goblet, in all directions),
a few guests dashed off to their studios to lock them,
and one woman, a "conceptual artist"
who had said my breathing while swimming
was "interesting" (she had crawled back and forth
along the pool's edge dunking her head
to listen "at ten-foot, half-minute intervals"),
dropped a fistful of dinner utensils
and cried, "My God, what if they stole *my* things!"
And a few, whose faces seemed to bob around me
like balloons, asked how I was feeling.

I said fine though I was not fine,
though not exactly because of the burglary.
I don't know how memory

shapes the present, and the present, memory;
but today, when I found these lines in my copy
of Hannah Arendt's *Thinking* (which I was reading then)
with my underscoring and stars in the margin—
"Solitude is being with oneself. Loneliness
is being with no one."— I felt again
a desolation I had almost forgotten.
At Yaddo I could hear it whisper
like the voice of another person
mocking all I said outwardly calm or kind,
and for months, teaching classes or at dinner with friends,
my mind might blank as if slammed
by a wave, and I'd struggle to pretend
I wasn't somersaulting underwater unable to breathe.
It now seems part of being crazy
not to ask for help or let anyone see,
but I felt happy alone in my studio
watching light striate in glyphs down the trees
and the leaves flashing their silver undersides
when a gust bobbed the branch-tips
to nod *all right, all right* like tired old men.
With a symphony on the stereo blended in,
inside this cube of light and music and weightless shadow,
being alive felt like a gift. It didn't matter
where it came from or who or what was the giver.

So I was sure the burglary
was a retraction. What an old story:
Lapsed Catholic Still Sees Through Lens of Religion:

29

if, for example, there's no actual Devil
he must be part of me. And so on.
But the shapes I saw are beautiful.
To offset *Thinking* I was reading Greek myths
that say that every god is both God and Devil;
that the gods are multiple and jealous;
that the impersonal, internal power balance on Olympus
determines our puny earthbound fates.
The puny burglary happened Saturday,
August fifteenth, during the Travers Stakes,
a festival day in Saratoga—except for the race,
not communal, but countless simultaneous days
running parallel on discrete economic levels
from high rollers in for the weekend to the locals.
The week previous I had met two blonde tipsy
doctors' wives slumming in a disco
who invited me and about forty-four others
to a huge party the night of the Travers.
On the way to that party I first saw my studio
after the burglary: it looked hardly disturbed but dead,
the corpse of a natural, expected death,
as if the typewriter, lamp, and stereo
had been the soul of a life
that could be snuffed so easily and quick.
They still held to their places as shadows.
In the corner, a stack of books that had been next to a speaker
was knocked over, probably by accident,
and the looseleaf notes crowning it scattered or flung.
The breeze through the gaping window and screen

barely raised the papers' edges,
like hems of a white-gowned chorus
at the cue to take a breath and sing.
I figured I shouldn't touch anything.
The window was the one I always looked through.
I had never seen the trees through a slashed screen.
Had I never been there at exactly this time?
The light was different. Everything had changed.

The detective copied serial numbers from packing boxes
but said I could go ahead and kiss my stuff goodbye.
I sat at the desk a minute while he left in his Chevy.
After dinner I went to the party anyway,
following a map on a "Mine Shaft" cocktail napkin
scrawled over a cartoon barmaid in a mining helmet
with tiny ballpoint x's for the houses
so it looked like she was wearing a barbed-wire crown,
and found the street encircling the golf course,
and the house x-ed into the mining helmet's beam.
The husband, as it happened, wasn't a doctor
but a dentist, and it wasn't a huge party
but a buffet supper for twenty.
He jerked his wife into the kitchen
and wanted to know who exactly I might be,
when in fact it was her friend, the other woman,
with whom I had gone out to the parking lot
to have a drink in her Cadillac,
whose dashboard glowed with digital readouts
when she switched the ignition to play the tape deck,

whose front seat moved electronically,
she told me, to one hundred and one different positions,
then flicked her tongue across her teeth,
which, in that green glow, were exceedingly white.
"My husband likes this car," she said. "I hate it."
Now we were chatting on her friend's sun deck—
almost a hazard where a fairway doglegged—
elbow to elbow, with chinette plates.
Ten feet off, with golf-shirted cronies,
her husband—also a dentist—kept one eye on me
as if he were passing an unlit alley.
Whether from loneliness or perversity,
I stayed, and, after less than twenty minutes,
became, amazingly, just one of the party,
TV maybe creating a new human ability
to absorb discordant information instantly
and go on smiling as if the fact weren't happening.
The guests were all dentists, their wives, and hygienists;
all had long been curious about Yaddo
which stands like a Vatican in their midst.
In twos and threes, all twenty of them talked to me
("You're a poet? What do you *do*?"),
and someone's unemployed kid brother
who could have passed for Arthur Bremer
recited his own personal poems to me
endlessly. I tilted my ear toward him and listened.
I thought this something I could do.
Maybe for this reason, if for no other,

everyone came to seem to feel pleasure
in my being there. I began enjoying myself, too,
until we heard, from the den this time,
the host dentist screaming at his wife:
"What the hell are you doing inviting to our *home*
some strange guy you meet in a bar?
To humiliate me? Or are you crazy?"
And everyone stopped their conversation
and looked in my direction. The voice in me
said *Stay. See what happens.* I knew where
it had come from. And I did stay there
a minute too long. In Mexico one time,
I was watching a movie in a neighborhood theatre
when a knife-blade slit the screen from behind.
I thought it must be an adolescent prank
until I heard over the sound track
someone not faking being stabbed and beaten.
The movie kept showing, shirts and hell shapes
flashing inside the shrieking black gash
while the audience exploded toward the exits.
(It turned out to be some dope lord's control tactics.)
Maybe my studio's slashed screen recalled it
without my knowing, because for that minute
I could still see all the guests looking at me
but on the deck with us was a vertical black cut.
Then it wasn't there. It wasn't. I put my drink down,
walked to the den, said I was very sorry, thanked them.
The two or three men who had followed me in

to make sure I was leaving and leaving quietly
and watched me back my car out of the driveway
looked like children at the window watching it rain.

I went back to "The Mine Shaft" then
and threw down shot after shot of bourbon
as a strobe underlighting the plastic multicolored dancefloor
hammered the dancers into fragments.
I didn't want to die. I wanted to be nothing.
But last call came, overhead lights slapped on,
the parking lot demolition derby began,
wheels burning rubber and furious chromed engines,
and the women who were still with friends
hooked arms to step briskly through dog packs of men
screaming furious invitations into their faces.
I drove back to my studio shouting nonsense,
snapped on the bare bulb on the ceiling,
and sat at my desk drinking six-packs watching
my redoubled reflections in fourteen black windows
until the dawn erased the faintest ones
and minute by minute they all faded to nothing.
At one point that night I talked to each in sequence,
spitting I don't know what insults, and they
talked back, came to life, told me off,
fourteen, fourteen hundred at once, until I found myself
speed-walking a circle around the room.
Anybody going by would have thought I was crazy
and I guess I *was* crazy, but I remember
I was trying to see myself as a stranger

by becoming person after person
I had talked to that day.

I had only a few more weeks at Yaddo.
Someone loaned me a typewriter. The lamp was replaced
by a silver architect's model that clamped to the desk.
Nobody had an extra stereo.
Before I could make myself sit in the studio
during the daylight for an hour or two,
the dentist's wife came to see me in her Cadillac,
which looked even more wacky in daytime
parking next to the used Subarus and Toyotas
of painters and composers. One by one,
I pulled the fourteen brittle yellow shades
down over the windows, and the light
turned the color of peach-meat.
She told me the host had stormed out
after I left the party, they didn't know if he was after me,
but he didn't come back all night
and he and her friend were getting a divorce.
I couldn't guess why she had come to tell me this.
What could I do about it? And we sat there
with not another word to say to each other,
me at the desk, her in the armchair.
So when she said finally,
"I really came to apologize for the party,"
I didn't reply: "Apologize? It was my fault."
Or: "*You* didn't do anything wrong."
Or: "That's not necessary" or "How kind."

But: "I really don't want to be part of all this,"
before it had even been in my mind.
"Of course. Why would you?" she said quickly,
softly, looking down, looking away.

But both of us knew here was no tragedy.
Neither of us could ever love the other.
Nothing called up our courage or honor.
Yet something began filling that room like water—
rust-color, thick as the merger of the slow orange light
and silence between us, or maybe it was the light
and silence becoming one thing apart from us,
apart from anyone or anything human.
I can't imagine what she felt except discomfort
and the generosity to part without meanness;
her eyes looked past me scanning the room
and the sudden pleasure on her face must have come from
her recalling what I had mentioned at the party
and thinking it a way to push through this embarrassment:
"Well, Michael," she said cheerily, "tell me about the burglary."
I couldn't tell her much, but I wanted to.

A SPLINTER

A twinge forgotten by the body
among its million daily nerve-firings;
and a moment uncolored by consciousness,

the thick paperback splayed
on your lap at the place you stopped
who knows what phantom universe

after Anna Karenina,
poisoned by poison–love,
throws herself under the iron horse

and you had been taken into her thinking
Where am I? What am I doing? Why?
She wanted to rise and draw back

but something enormous and implacable
struck her head and dragged her along.
"Oh Lord, forgive me all my sins!" she

screams as the tall wheels
crush and split her silk dress,
ravenous flesh, and delicate skeleton.

In the station on the platform
you turned away
from her pain finally done

and laid the book down.
The mind, released then,
began to fill with its native emptiness,

idle thoughts darting
like translucent minnows in a clear shallow.
You lifted your hand to gaze

with wonder at the palm and fingers
as if they weren't your own,
as you have since childhood

how many times, and noticed
a splinter under a fingertip
and began digging through the skin for it

with fingernails then a nailfile
then a cuticle scissors until you bled
and it slid out, impaled softwood,

moist, black as an eyelash,
and you came back to your own life
crying not for yourself.

ONE

. . . *six million dead,*
a million of them children.

A ten-year-old
in a crinoline, her neck
inclined like a bather
by Degas, her washed black
hair spilling forward
over her crown and forehead
because the sheep shears
has begun to clip at her nape,
and for this split second
the first puffball of hair
balances on the unearthly
blue-white knuckles of the hand
about to drive these clippers
up her skull. This image
from nowhere particular—
books or movies or newspaper
stories—caught in a gauze
of grayness and cold,
did it ever really happen
to *this* little girl,
the wispy hollow at the base
of *her* skull shocked
by freezing stainless steel?
I have to think
to follow from the hand
up the emblazoned sleeve,
to see the ovens in the background,
to imagine what I can't
imagine but can only name:

her mother's anguish,
her father's nightmare terror
ensnarled with their fear
for themselves and for each other—
has she lost them already
or are they watching her?
There must have been soldiers
whose Nazi blinders
were seared through by the horror,
but all I see of them
in this split second
are blue-white knuckles
working an implement
used on animals
on this little girl
who dressed last night for a party,
and now, too confused to cry,
stands somewhere amid
barbed wire and mud
her head being shaved.

COUNTY FAIR

Almost anyone, I guess, can rent booth-space,
but this year whoever assigned it
thinks in odd logic: Planned Parenthood
with its calmly catastrophic population charts
squeezed between Right-to-Life
posters of bloody embryos screaming MURDER
and Mary Kay Cosmetics' amazing-one-time offer
for a fabulous-free-complete makeover.
On the way there in our red sports car
that topped a hundred thousand miles this summer
and now rattles like a fossil, you said,
"We were going to talk again in a week
about having kids. It's been two weeks."—
not saying each week we wait
means more risk, physical risk,
unlike my fear, airy and ineffable.
Above the wind and clunking universal joint,
I caught the moon rising in a sky
of clear steel blue, and tried to describe to you
the hawks I had seen that afternoon
gliding on the air-drafts.
They were so still with their wings stretched
they looked like vicious insignia
on some robber baron's escutcheon,
and they circled for so long—three of them—
I half began to think I was the one
they were hunting. Any minute, I thought,
they'll tuck their wings and plummet,
but the death it meant, that caught my throat,

41

wasn't mine but yours, and I snapped back to daylight
inside a glimmer of what that would feel like,
and when I found you weeding the garden
you looked up and asked, "What's happened?"

There didn't seem to be a single couple
on the fairgrounds with less than six children
under ten, or three under five,
or an infant in arms and themselves
still children, starch-fat and dirt-poor,
bobbling loads of midway junk,
clumps of fried dough, corn dogs on sticks,
drifting by pitchmen's gravelly raps,
grinning or yawning, maybe forgetting a minute
the bills, the bounced check, the food stamps.
We rested on a bench, muted because of them,
ignoring for a minute the clamor of our own wants.
A bunch of pre-teens from a local dance school
in lamé tights and glittered nails and faces
began a chorus line on a plywood platform
as a pair of archaic bell-shaped speakers
popped and crackled "Girls Just Want To Have Fun."
Steps half-matched, twirls begun too late,
it was less like dancing than a forced march–in–place
sort–of–in–time to the banging cadence of the music.
The mothers who had helped them practice
for months in front of every mirror in the house
were easy to pick out. They were marching, too,
almost imperceptibly, mouthing a song

one of them might remember
without knowing where it came from
out on her evening walk or watering the lawn
when her daughter has grown daughters
already starting families of their own.
"You forgot your free makeover," I said driving home,
and, smiling, you reached over and pinned my hand to the horn.

PORTRAIT OF A LADY

". . . because she was in that state
so many young girls go through—
a state of sexual obsession that can be
like a sort of trance."
　　　　　　　—Doris Lessing

Was it only the new old chemical stirrings
that made her shoplift purple corduroys
and squeeze into them out of her mother's hearing
to discover what noises could come from boys?

"Like sleepwalking on stilts," she laughed years later
about the cheap spiked heels wobbling under her feet.
The lip-smacks and wolf-whistles she remembered
as fainter than the slamming of her own heartbeat

when she appeared to herself in the overlit mirror
that Saturday afternoon in the shopping mall john.
All the stoned girls quit primping and stared.
And time stopped. Then one stuck out her tongue.

Our lady flipped that little whiffet the finger
and spent her strength to yank open the door
and promenade bravely past Sears and What-A-Burger
down the white-hot, phosphorescent corridor

to draw a boy to her who would answer her anger.
Of course what she got was bruises from their pawing,
fast rides, dirty jokes, and thorough ignorance of her.
But how could she stop this feeling of gnawing?

One day she saw the answer playing Space Invaders.
His fury charged his body like a thick, hot wire.

And she'd meet him there and do anything he told her
until for no reason he didn't show up anymore.

This is the time she marked as her awakening:
the slow hours picking through the heart's rubble
and finding only bits of incomprehensible pain.
Then *she* broke hearts, got a teacher in trouble,

and never gave herself wholly to anyone again.
But cruelty was a drug she needed less with age.
She lived calmly with a husband and children
and her body locked around her like a cage.

FIRST EXERCISE

I was swimming
because I wanted to get skinny,
having passed the age of thirty
when the body begins its gradual revenge
for all those days of inattention
it secretly begrudged all along.
So I was finally paying it my full attention,
pulling it as I could back and forth
across the pool's width at the baby end;
standing after each lap to wait for breath
and study the excellent rhythms of the swimmers
in the roped lanes of the Olympic pool adjoining
as the light through high, leaded windows
broke into diamonds off their wakes;
nodding in turn to my companions at this end:
two impossibly vigorous, white-capped old men
and a dark woman in a black spandex suit
that fit her like skin. I've always hated swimming
for impeccable reasons, especially since
I'm nearly blind without my contact lenses,
and I didn't understand the new goggles
I bought for my new regimen did not mean
I could keep my lenses in and see new things;
so from one of my fancy underwater racing turns
I came up without them,
and touched my eyes, and looked, and felt
a rush of panic into my chest,
the shock when someone says
there's been a terrible accident

and you don't know who or what.
Of course, after a second, I thought
"It's only your contact lenses,"
but I dived for them anyway again and again,
trying to hold myself under to pet the tile
with my palms, and later, as I walked home,
the world a blur of dull color run together,
I thought of my friend diving at dusk
in that mountain lake for his daughter
and what came to him when his hands
sank into the cold mud at the bottom.

BLUE CORRIDOR

When I hung up, it was like
a blue corridor. I couldn't see you
anymore. And my stomach
kept wanting to get hurt, to be
able to say *I'm sick*.

Blue corridor where I smelled death
fly past, its push of bad air
as from an open mouth.
Something you said had me
thinking of it, I guess,

but even earlier, before you called,
I had been on the street at dusk,
when the first few cars
flash on their lights, and realized
a day had passed again without you,

another day that was easy enough
except for this moment when I looked
and the street was a blue corridor,
no cars the length of it, no lights,
only tinged air, and you not here.

THE DITCH

In the ditch, half-ton sections of cast-iron molds
hand-greased at the seams with pale petroleum waste
and screw-clamped into five-hundred-gallon cylinders
drummed with rubber-headed sledges inside and out
to settle tight the wet concrete
that, dried and caulked, became Monarch Septic Tanks;
and, across the ditch, my high school football coach,
Don Compo, spunky pug of a man,
bronze and bald, all biceps and pecs,
raging at some "attitude" of mine
he snipped from our argument about Vietnam—
I mean *raging,* scarlet, veins bulging from his neck,
he looked like a hard-on stalking back and forth—
but I had started college, this was a summer job,
I no longer had to take his self-righteous, hectoring shit,
so I was chuckling merrily, saying he was ludicrous,
and he was calling me "College Man Ryan"
and with his steel-toed workboot kicking dirt
that clattered against the molds and puffed up between us.

It's probably not like this anymore, but every coach
in my hometown was a lunatic. Each had different quirks
we mimicked, beloved bromides whose parodies we intoned,
but they all conducted practice like bootcamp,
the same tirades and abuse, no matter the sport,
the next game the next battle in a neverending war.
Ex-paratroopers and -frogmen, at least three
finally-convicted child molesters, genuine sadists
fixated on the Commie menace and our American softness

49

that was personally bringing the country to the brink of collapse—
in this company, Don Compo didn't even seem crazy.
He had never touched any of us;
his violence was verbal, which we were used to,
having gotten it from our fathers
and given it back to our brothers and to one another
since we had been old enough to button our own pants.
Any minute—no guessing what might spring it—
he could be butting your face-mask and barking up your nostrils,
but generally he favored an unruffled, moralistic carping
in which I, happy to spot phoniness,
saw pride and bitterness masquerading as teaching.
In the locker-room, I'd sit where I could roll my eyeballs
as he droned, but, across the ditch,
he wasn't lecturing, but fuming, flaring
as I had never seen in four years of football,
and it scared and thrilled me to defy him and mock him
when he couldn't make me handwash jockstraps after practice
or do pushups on my fingertips in a mud puddle.

But it was myself I was taunting. I could see my retorts
snowballing toward his threat to leap the ditch
and beat me to a puddle of piss ("you craphead,
you wiseass"), and my unspading a shovel from a dirt pile
and grasping its balance deliberately down the handle
and inviting him to try it.
Had he come I would have hit him.
There's no question about that.
For a moment, it ripped through our bewilderment

which then closed over again
like the ocean
if a cast-iron mold were dropped in.
I was fired when the boss broke the tableau.
"The rest of you," he said, "have work to do,"
and, grabbing a hammer and chisel, Don Compo
mounted the mold between us in the ditch
and with one short punch split it down the seam.

SMOKE

There was a woman whose husband had died,
the mother of one of my sister's friends,
we took her to lunch when a few weeks
had gone by, she sat in the back
between my sister and me the whole way there
dress up to her thighs, leg flush against mine,
chatting to my parents in the front seat
about her plans to move away, and when I
held the car door for her, she slid out slowly,
one leg at a time, so I'd see the plump silk
underneath, then grazed me so lightly
as she stood up I was never sure
if she had touched me or not.

And what of it?
What of a secret that takes you, to which
you give yourself, that stays with you,
to which you return as to a pleasure
in a drawer, until some remote
future afternoon when it's there again
after not being with you for such a long time
you can't remember when it was forgotten?
When I lay down for a nap today
the light softened
as if the windows were being smeared with vaseline
and a fantasy began that I like
but I thought no, I always have this,

what about another, one I used to have,
and there was the woman whose husband had died
and my life in the world seemed made of smoke.

HOUSEFLIES

It's not them that make me crazy
but they seem the essence of madness,
ramming the window headfirst
yet clicking like fingernails on the glass.

In this disproportionate quiet,
with old newspapers rolled in my fist,
I wait one by one when they light
for their hairspring legs to relax,

which means their insect attention
has shifted wrongly
from the danger of death,
and they are probably lucky

they don't get a chance to reflect
on how they acquired bad instinct
before my bludgeon of published disasters
turns them each to a pinch of smash.

But they must have a nest in the woodwork.
When the sun makes my window hot
they are always there pressing on it,
the same eight thick black knots.

LARKINESQUE

Reading in the paper a summary
of a five-year psychological study
that shows those perceived as most beautiful
are treated differently,

I think *they could have just asked me,*
remembering a kind of pudgy kid
and late puberty, the bloody noses
and wisecracks because I wore glasses,

though we all know by now how awful it is
for the busty starlet no one takes seriously,
the loveliest women I've lunched with
lamenting the opacity of the body,

they can never trust a man's interest
even when he seems not just out for sex
(eyes focus on me above rim of wineglass),
and who *would* want to live like this?

And what does beauty do to a man?—
Don Juan, Casanova, Lord Byron—
those fiery eyes and steel jawlines
can front a furnace of self-loathing,

all those breathless women rushing to him,
while hubby's at the office or ball game,
primed to be consumed by his beauty
while he stands next to it, watching.

So maybe the looks we're dealt are best.
It's only common sense that happiness
depends on some bearable deprivation
or defect, and who knows what conflicts

great beauty could have caused,
what cruelties one might have suffered
from those now friends, what unmanageable
possibilities smiling at every small turn?

So if I get up to draw a tumbler
of ordinary tap water and think *what if this were
nectar dripping from delicious burning fingers,*
will all I've missed knock me senseless?

No. Of course not. It won't.

THE CROWN OF FROGS

In Bertolucci's *1900,* half-brothers—
the son and bastard son of an estate owner—
are born in the same hour and grow up
together, learning as they grow older
the difference between them, the one.
being groomed with education for power
while the other is worked all day like an animal
then left on his own to roam the farm.

They realize that they have changed,
changed from mirrors to shadows of each other,
when the rich son finds the poor one
snatching frogs from a stream and stringing them
around the crown of his hat onto a circular wire
that twangs apart each time he flicks
the hook and eyelet at his temple
like the trigger of some homemade gun.

No one hears the sound but him.
It's snuffed on the sound track under their soprano Italian
and the crystalline, shade-dappled, ankle-deep water
gurgling over the rocks. The crown of frogs
above his Huck Finn face fills the screen
as he talks, as he mocks rich-boy clumsiness
then cuffs the water and jams another frog onto the wire
without breaking the flow of his abuse,

he has become so expert practicing on himself
in the hours he has been given to waste.

57

The frogs are his bitterness incarnate, his brain
turned inside out, squirming, bleeding
in trickles where the wire threads the gills,
one leg or two or ten abruptly straightened
as if a shock circled the wire
down into these pale underbellies of despair

bloating and releasing the air
in great sighs, in hopeless torpor.
Twenty years later a fascist monster
rapes another little boy in a cellar
and swings him by his heels into a wall
in a scene that, to me, is film's most sickening:
knickers tangle at the ankles
as offscreen his head thuds, and thuds again,

and, though who can bear it?, thuds a final time
before the legs go white and lifeless.
Neither brother becomes that murderer,
but I walked from the theater stunned
into a forgotten Florida afternoon
with my dad's new boss's son
who was exactly my age, the age
of the children in the film, eight or nine.

For weeks beforehand I had been warned
to be nice to him, and while our parents
lounged on the patio with Windex-blue drinks
he took me out beyond the fence

of his vast backyard to his secret place
where he had strung a wire clothesline
between two palmettos, and in the marsh grass underneath
had stashed a clutch of bamboo poles

with tiny wire nooses attached.
"These are the prisoners," he announced,
and from the marsh grass he produced
a valentine candy-box crossed with rubberbands
and icepick holes in each chamber of the heart.
"And that's the graveyard," pointing to a plot
of turned earth all slimy and wet.
"Do you want to see one hung?"

I said *what hung* but he couldn't hear me then.
His eyes glazed as he probed two fingers into the box
and brought to within an inch of my nose
a buttery, brown, tiger-striped toad
squeezed so tightly in his fist
I was afraid its head would pop off like a cork.
Then he looped it in a noose
and cast it over the clothesline.

"Watch it *piss!*" he screeched, and, as the toad
twisted and swung, the needle-stream
cut the air into patterns of contorted diamonds,
and he wheezed "Hee . . . hee . . . hee . . ."
unable to breathe until the toad
choked and swayed to rest and hung

59

plumb and quiet for that endless minute.
Then he buried it and dug some others up.

The toad instead of himself: it now seems obvious.
His unspeakable language now seems obvious.
Even then I knew I had been a witness to madness
and after I talked him back to the house,
swearing to share his secret with no one else,
my mother held out her hand to me
to step back up onto a patio
that felt like an ice floe on a sea of oil.

But life's not like the movies.
That afternoon nothing changed dramatically.
We weren't swept into a terrible current of history.
Should the sky have rained fire and the earth
opened in outrage? We all just sat there
on our loungers until evening—two silent little boys,
one crazy, and four adults: soft, pale people
in black elastic knee socks and plaid Bermuda shorts.

PASSION

Chilly early Saturday, my study
its usual chaos: a cluster of half-digested paperbacks
around the stuffed chair and floorlamp
thinning to the rug's periphery
like a molecule's probability graph;
stacks of drafts for this or that poem
or essay, flashes temporarily shaped
into one of a trillion possible embodiments,
encrusted now before a wicker wastebasket
erupting months of slamdunked crumpled
legal sheets and looseleaf; and me—
happy after waking next to you—
diffused through this minuscule universe,
a larger but less cohesive bit of matter
than the poster of the pre-Columbian
fertility goddess staring at no one
from above the desk. I'm writing this,
for instance, because Maria Rodriguez
beams from the pile of old Sunday *Times*
I twist into knots for kindling
to get my wood stove going in the morning.
She's hugging the man she married
at San Quentin the moment the photo
was taken, where marriages are performed
in the hospitality room the first Tuesday
every month, where this month (June, 1982)
there were eleven. For a few minutes
I sit crosslegged before the stove's mouth
and try to ride with her on the free bus

for convicts' families from Los Angeles—
squabbling toddlers, rap music pumping
from a boom box, her heels and dress tucked
in an overnight case on the overhead rack
with the pearl eyeshadow she'll redo one last time
in the video-scanned hospitality room
before her man appears behind the glass partition
and floats like that, ghostly, in her mind
as she changes back afterwards into her everyday clothes
for the night ride home. Maria Rodriguez
says her friends tell her she's crazy,
and her family, forget it, none of them
would come. Statistics prove these marriages
collapse after the prisoner's released,
but it's not for then she's marrying.
It's for this passion
she had only dreamed, that she thought
happened only in movies and never believed
could be real. I believe it's real.
I remember us trying to talk about it
the day the article was published.
Passio, "suffering; Christ's scourging
and crucifixion," the Latin
from the Indo-European root for *harm*
from which also comes Greek for *destruction.*
As you read me the etymology, it melted
easily into the sacred music of Scarlatti
and aroma of coffee and bacon
that swell our home on Sunday mornings

when love seems uncomplicated and kind.
I don't remember what I said or did
the rest of that day—worked in here probably,
read the paper, watched baseball on TV—
but this morning, knotting this page for the fire,
I thought of keeping it, I thought
of clipping the photo of Maria Rodriguez
and tacking it in here so she would tell me
if I forget what passion means,
I thought of it, then jammed it
into the stove and gave it to the flames.

PEDESTRIAN PASTORAL

It's nothing to a squirrel
to vault ten times its pulsing length
and come down running on a branch
thin as a popsicle,

and much less to a groundhog
flattened by a tire
to hold one perfect paw in air
as if summoning a partner,

and this unexpectedly gorgeous
shaggy white cow, inexplicably
alone in a pasture—
what is it to her this December

if at her black nose breath-puffs
vanish and appear like a Don't Walk
warning blinker? But I do walk
happily in this mild Virginia winter

unable to feel absolutely sure
I won't be here forever
almost like this, a pure observer,
for once oblivious

to the spurs of ego and desire
that—whatever death is
or is not—could be paradise
to finally do without.

MOONLIGHT

It silvers the lawn,
its off-white wash tingeing
these hours alone,
frozen dewdropped grassblades
an army of sparklers
I would love like Walt Whitman
to insinuate myself among,
drawing them out about home
before I write their letters for them
and dress the gangrenous wounds
they will soon die from,
petting the feverish ones,
kissing one or two of them
open-mouthed, long, and lingering,
my gift-satchel emptied,
my heart broken.
If you were beside me, you'd say,
"It looks like snow, only invisible,"
and the world moonlight makes,
in which even roof-tin
glints like platinum, could seem
a distillation of joyous thought,
all clarity and outline,
the great winter-stripped maple
you married me under in summer
flaring its black skeleton against the sky
as I walk straight for it
praying for no more words between us
that are killing everything.

FIRE

I think of myself as dust of bones
mornings when I awake
to find the fine white ash
lining the bottom of my box stove.
Each night I slide in
logs thicker than the circle
of my thigh, and watch them all
blaze for a while,
because I'm about to sleep
and know that what I'll see encircles me
as if I were having no dream
but it is having me.
With the fire, in the darkened room,
my life begins not to be my own,
a pulse of watery blue transparencies
inside the jagged flames
that die and flare again
while on the underside begin
orange coals that should seem
so cool and delicious on the tongue,
and all of it nothing by morning.

TOURISTS ON PAROS

If I die or something happens to us
and a stray breeze the length of the house
takes you alone back to that June on Paros
when we wrote every morning in a whitewashed room
then lay naked in the sun all afternoon
and came back at dusk famished for each other
and talked away the night in a taverna by the water—
I hope the memory gives you nothing but pleasure.

But if you also suddenly feel the loss
snap open beneath like a well covered with grass,
remember our stumbling in T-shirts and shorts
onto that funeral party in the café at breakfast:
not the widow, barely sixteen, in harsh wool cloth
nor the grief that filled the air and seemed boundless,

but the brawny, red-haired Orthodox priest
whose shaggy orange beard over his black-smocked chest
was like an explosion from a dark doorway
of a wild, high-pitched laugh.

CROSSROADS INN

October 25, 1983

Sitting on a rock
as someone might have done
two hundred years ago
next to this fire-brick tavern,

I can feel the Virginia hills
surge up to my feet.
They are like waves stopped still.
In the declivities between,

an asphalt strip of road
curls and disappears,
and a vulture is overhead
climbing, pumping the air

with earnest, floppy strokes
beneath black hawks that ride
the high currents like smoke.
And something turns in my mind

when I follow the road below
as far as I can see:
two hundred years ago,
needing rest and company,

a drover walking livestock
to a nearby river port
stopped here overnight
and in the evening sat on this rock

thinking *What will be here*
two hundred years from now
and the surging hills answered
Nothing that you know.

A POSTCARD FROM ITALY

I can't tell you how beautiful
is the flowering of water
in this park in Florence
on Sunday afternoon in October,
but a rusty cluster of nozzles
fires water-jets toward the sun
in arcs that land as a star-shape
on a little circular pond
defined by white stones
and diffused by white swans.
And everyone stopping
different trouble in different lives
may share for a while
this spectacular calm—
this patter of water, gray shade
of evergreens, and always amazing
slow gliding of the swans.
I know the photos of teenagers
taking one another's pictures
mugging in the crotch
of an ancient, gnarled cedar
may be found years from now in a shoebox
by someone to whom they mean nothing,
and the innocence of children
whipping around the pond
in rented push-pedal carts
might become some greedy adult obsession,
but this old woman in black
who had been walking here

with her hands clasped behind her neck
like a prisoner
just threw back her head to stretch
her palms toward the sun,
and I wish somehow you could see her.

STONE PAPERWEIGHT

I was napping as usual
between our dinner and your bedtime
so I would be alert working
in the timeless hours before dawn

in which I become almost bodiless
because the world has black gloves on
its touching agonies and beauties
and leaves me happily alone—

when you broke into my dream
before I woke with your lying down
freshly naked against me
in flesh cool as the stone

I was dreaming you found at a shoreline,
worn flawless by water and sand,
and gave me to weight my papers
against the disturbing wind.

GOD HUNGER

When the immutable accidents of birth—
parentage, hometown, all the rest—
no longer anchor this fiction of the self
and its incessant *I me mine,*

then words won't be like nerves in a stump
crackling with messages that end up nowhere,
and I'll put on the wind like a gown of light linen
and go be a king in a field of weeds.

TANGLEWOOD

for H

We were trying to talk about love,
and blank pain that stays blank
until music makes a shape for it,
so to know it, so to feel it out,
when you said, "Look, we've joined a swarm!"—
we had become another couple among hundreds
converging to get in, hand in hand, blankets
under arms, wine bottles swinging by the necks
like pendulums of old clocks. You said,
"Let's try not to talk until the music's over,"

but when it began, and the light was almost gone,
someone showed us how she loved a man
the way her back inclined sitting next to him,
the way her hand traveled his back and neck
as if there were no limits to her touch,
as if there had been no boundaries drawn
and she believed she had found the one
from whom to take essential sustenance
and felt no need to seek it anywhere else.
You said, "I've never felt that way myself."

And then, "Maybe it can happen
for only a few moments in a life."
All the other couples near our blanket
had made other arrangements, upright
in lawn chairs or scattered on the grass.
One man curled up with his back to his wife,
his head pillowed on the inside of his wrist,

while she sat hugging her knees to her chest
as if they had argued to exhaustion,
and just switched off the light.

But soon you were drawn inside the music.
The air suffused with music and you breathed it.
Darkness thickened so those surrounding
became black cutouts melded or apart.
You lay back, eyes wide, listening hard,
to watch the crossing of the music and the stars,
to feel yourself nothing but some chance meeting
of endless space and endless inwardness,
to float if only a minute with the music
over touches useless, and tender, and electric.

SWITCHBLADE

Most of the past is lost,
and I'm glad mine has vanished
into blackness or space or whatever nowhere
what we feel and do goes,
but there were a few cool Sunday afternoons
when my father wasn't sick with hangover
and the air in the house wasn't foul with anger
and the best china had been cleared after the week's best meal
so he could place on the table his violins
to polish with their special cloth and oil.
Three violins he'd arrange
side by side in their velvet-lined cases
with enough room between for the lids to lie open.
They looked like children in coffins,
three infant sisters whose hearts had stopped for no reason,
but after he rubbed up their scrolls and waists
along the lines of the grain to the highest sheen,
they took on the knowing posture of women in silk gowns
in magazine ads for new cars and ocean voyages,
and, as if a violin were a car in storage
that needed a spin around the block every so often,
for fifteen minutes he would play each one—
though not until each horsehair bow was precisely tightened
and coated with rosin, and we had undergone an eon of tuning.
When he played no one was allowed to speak to him.
He seemed to see something drastic across the room
or feel it through his handkerchief padding the chinboard.
So we'd hop in front of him waving or making pig-noses

the way kids do to guards at Buckingham Palace,
and after he had finished playing and had returned to himself,
he'd softly curse the idiocy of his children
beneath my mother's voice yelling to him from the kitchen
That was beautiful, Paul, play it again.

He never did, and I always hoped he wouldn't,
because the whole time I was waiting for his switchblade
to appear, and the new stories he'd tell me
for the scar thin as a seam
up the white underside of his forearm,
for the chunks of proud flesh on his back and belly,
scarlet souvenirs of East St. Louis dance halls in the twenties,
cornered in men's rooms, ganged in blind alleys,
always slashing out alone with this knife.
First the violins had to be snug again
inside their black cases
for who knew how many more months or years or lifetimes;
then he had to pretend to have forgotten
why I was sitting there wide-eyed across from him
long after my sister and brother had gone off with friends.
Every time, as if only an afterthought,
he'd sneak into his pocket and ease the switchblade
onto the bare table between us,
its thumb-button jutting from the pearl-and-silver plating
like the eye of some sleek prehistoric fish.
I must have known it wouldn't come to life
and slither toward me by itself,

but when he'd finally nod to me to take it
its touch was still warm with his body heat
and I could feel the blade inside aching
to flash open with the terrible click
that sounds now like just a *tsk* of disappointment,
it has become so sweet and quiet.